THE FRIENDLY STRANGER

Written by Margaret Williams
Illustrated by Steve Smallman

CANDLE
BOOKS

Written by Margaret Williams
Illustrated by Steve Smallman
Copyright © 2006 Lion Hudson plc/Tim Dowley and
Peter Wyart trading as Three's Company

Published in 2006 by Candle Books
(a publishing imprint of Lion Hudson plc).

Distributed in the UK by Marston Book Services Ltd,
PO Box 269, Abingdon, Oxon OX14 4YN

Distributed in the USA by Kregel Publications,
Grand Rapids, Michigan 49501

UK   ISBN-13: 978-1-85985-630-7
        ISBN-10: 1-85985-630-6

USA ISBN-13: 978-0-8254-7317-3
        ISBN-10: 0-8254-7317-9

Worldwide co-edition produced by
Lion Hudson plc, Mayfield House
256 Banbury Road
Oxford, OX2 7DH, England
Tel: +44 (0) 1865 302750
Fax: +44 (0) 1865 302757
email: coed@lionhudson.com
www.lionhudson.com

Printed in China

There was once a man who had to travel from Jerusalem to Jericho.

He packed his bags, and set out early.
But the road got steeper, the sun grew hotter…

and the rocks beside the road
seemed to grow bigger.

By midday the sun was burning hot.
But the man dare not stop for fear he
wouldn't arrive in Jericho before nightfall.
He plodded on.

Suddenly there was a shout.
Before the man knew it,
robbers leapt from the rocks.
They stole his bags and his best coat.
Then they ran off.

The poor man lay on the road.
His head ached. What was he to do?

All he could hear was a grasshopper squeaking.

Then he heard *flip-flop, flip-flop*.
He lifted his head.
Was someone coming?
Yes! It was a priest walking to Jerusalem.

The poor man called out, "Help! Help!"
But when the priest saw him…

he crossed the road and walked on.
Flip-flop, flip flop. He disappeared
into the distance.

The man lay still again.
Then he heard *clomp-clomp, clomp-clomp*.
Was anyone there?
Yes! Someone else was on his way to Jerusalem.

This time it was a Very Important Person
from the temple.
And he was late!

The injured man called out, "Help! Help!"
The Very Important Person looked around in fright.
Then, he too crossed over and walked even faster!
Clomp-clomp-clomp-clomp-clomp-clomp.
Straight past the poor man.

No one else would come down the road now,
thought the man. The sun sank in the sky.
The man lay still.

Then he heard *clip-clop, clip-clop*.

It was a stranger with his donkey.
A stranger from an enemy country.
He certainly won't stop, thought the man.

But when the stranger reached the man,
he shouted "*Whoa!*" to his donkey.
He walked over.
"What happened?" he asked kindly.
"You look to be in a bad way."

The man explained that he had
been set on by robbers.
The stranger brought bandages
and oil and bathed his wounds.

Then he lifted the hurt man
onto his donkey's back.

Then they went on, ever so carefully.

At last they reached a house.
"Look after my friend," the stranger said.
"Take this money and make sure he has
food and medicine."

Jesus told this story about the stranger who helped.

Jesus said we should help *anyone* who needs us –
not just our friends.

You can read this story in your Bible in Luke 10:25-37

Water Stories
Adventures Afloat

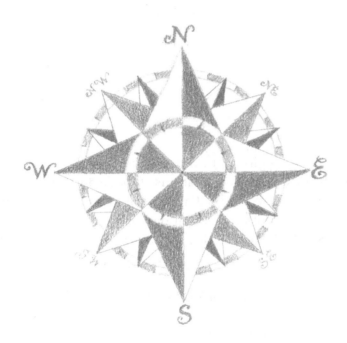

Written and illustrated
by Jim Arnosky

SEYMOUR SCIENCE
An Imprint of StarWalk Kids Media

This book is dedicated
to
John Nute

Published by Seymour Science
Except in the case of brief quotations embodied in critical reviews
and articles, no part of this book may be used or reproduced in any
manner whatsoever without written permission from the publisher.
Contact: StarWalk Kids Media, 15 Cutter Mill Road, Suite 242,
Great Neck, NY 11021

www.StarWalkKids.com

ISBN 978-1-623348-39-7

SEYMOUR SCIENCE
An Imprint of StarWalk Kids Media

Contents

Introduction

I am a water person. In the forest, I follow the sounds made by water tumbling over the stones and pebbles in a brook. On a beach, I thrill to the roar of a breaking wave and run to feel it wash ashore, cool around my legs. I wade and watch the different ways light plays on the water's surface. I swim and snorkel to see the way light penetrates the water in a dazzling curtain of individual rays. I like being surrounded by water; traveling in a ship crossing from land to land, or in a small boat that can go wherever the water goes.

My mate Deanna and I have floated on boats to many beautifully wild and mysterious watery places. Our shared boating life has been a series of small voyages, freshwater and saltwater, in rafts, canoes, kayaks, skiffs, sailboats, and cruisers we have owned, loved, and cared for. There have also been many hours spent aboard ferries, tugboats, trawlers, shrimp boats, glass bottom and offshore fishing vessels to get us someplace on the water, always to bring us closer to the aquatic and marine animals whose lives we find endlessly fascinating.

This book is a collection of stories about our home waters, which we know by heart, and distant waters that we wanted to explore. Some of these voyages encompassed more than a few days on the water. Others, only a few hours. All were true life adventures afloat.

Jim Arnosky

1.

Kayaking through the Mangrove Jungle

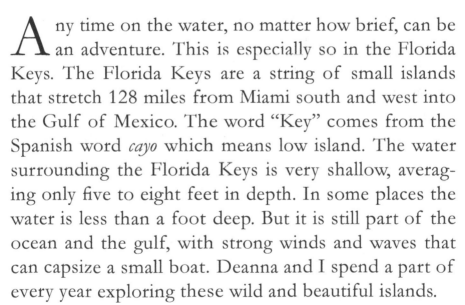

Any time on the water, no matter how brief, can be an adventure. This is especially so in the Florida Keys. The Florida Keys are a string of small islands that stretch 128 miles from Miami south and west into the Gulf of Mexico. The word "Key" comes from the Spanish word *cayo* which means low island. The water surrounding the Florida Keys is very shallow, averaging only five to eight feet in depth. In some places the water is less than a foot deep. But it is still part of the ocean and the gulf, with strong winds and waves that can capsize a small boat. Deanna and I spend a part of every year exploring these wild and beautiful islands.

I wanted to explore a narrow channel that cut through a particularly dense jungle of mangroves. Mangroves are small coastal trees that grow out of the salty water and stand up on their sturdy roots. Mangrove roots make me think of long fingers reaching underwater and clutching the soft bottom. There is no land, just roots, and on those roots live colorful little crabs and snails and beautiful, bright orange mangrove water snakes. Brown pelicans perch on the tops of the trees. Little brown lizards leap from stem to stem. Big green iguanas crawl on the branches. Golden orb weaver spiders stretch their webs from one waxy mangrove leaf to another. Sure-footed raccoons make their way over the slippery roots, following trails known only to them. Underwater, in the submerged tangle of roots, live dozens of species of small fish. And the narrow channels that wind through the mangrove jungle are used by sea turtles, sharks, dolphins, and rays traveling from bay to bay.

In order to get to the channel I wanted to explore, we would have to cross a long stretch of wide open water where a sudden change of wind or waves could flip our light canoe. Deanna and I decided to make the voyage on a kayak instead. Like a canoe, a kayak is a long boat of Native American invention. But where a canoe floats high on the water, the hull of a kayak sits low, hugging the water and holding the boat firmly down with suction. This suction makes a kayak track through wind and ocean waves much better than a canoe.

Since it was our first time in a kayak, it took some getting used to. But as we got into the rhythm of paddling the long narrow boat, we became more and more comfortable. Our new kayak, *Waterbird*, is actually a kayak/

canoe hybrid. It sits low in the water so that it handles
in the wind and waves like a kayak. And its open length
allows us to use it the way we use a canoe—with con-
siderable storage space between the front and back seats.
In the mangroves, the kayak's low profile was great for

sliding under the many branches hanging over the water.
And wherever we came to a wide lagoon where the wind
whipped the waves, the kayak hugged the water and kept
us on course without our having to paddle harder. But
sitting essentially down on the floor instead of on a high
canoe seat, combined with the kayak's extremely low freeboard (the distance from the water to the boat's gunwale),
put us very close to the water. And knowing that hammer-
head and bull sharks, large eagle rays, and big loggerhead
turtles regularly used the channels made being only inches
away from the water's surface unnerving, especially when
the kayak, which was much "tippier" than a canoe, would
roll from side to side whenever Deanna or I would momentarily fall out of sync with our paddling.

As we paddled down a long straight channel in the heart of the mangrove jungle, we came upon a dozen or so ramshackle houseboats, tied in a row to the mangrove roots and well hidden by the lush growth of mangrove leaves. People were living in the houseboats but those who were out on deck didn't speak to us as we passed. This is often the way with people who live on the water. They keep to themselves. Just beyond the houseboats, Deanna spotted a yellow-crowned night heron perched on the curve of a root. The nocturnal bird's big red eyes were partially closed. Deanna snapped a digital photo of the sleepy-looking bird winking at her as we glided by. We paddled deeper and deeper into the jungle of water and trees, following the many twists and turns of the wilderness waterway. Where the channel finally began to narrow to a dead end, I spotted something in the water ahead that made me stop paddling and speak softly for Deanna to halt as well.

At the edge of the mangroves, about two hundred feet from our boat, there appeared to be a large rough-barked log, floating. But there are no large or rough-barked trees in a mangrove jungle and no reason for such a log to be there, deep within the maze of tangled roots. We paddled a little closer, but being unsure of what we were approaching made us feel less and less secure in our movements. The kayak rocked, becoming uncomfortably tippy, and the surface of the water seemed even more dangerously close. We stopped paddling to let the kayak stabilize and glide on its own momentum toward the object ahead, closer and closer. Suddenly, I realized that the log was not a log. It was a crocodile—two feet wide and easily nine feet long! And it was keenly eyeballing our quickly approaching kayak.

By the time I squeaked out a frightened warning "Croc!" Deanna, who was in the bow of the boat and six feet closer to the creature, had already begun frantically paddling backward. Together, we managed to turn the kayak sideways just a few yards away from the big croc and then, dipping our paddles very quietly so as not to further alarm the enormous reptile, we watched anxiously to see what it would do. Would it swim away or swim toward us? Both Deanna and I kept our paddles in the water, ready to power out of there if we had to. But the crocodile simply stayed where it was, reclosed its eyes and continued soaking in the sun that shined more generously through the canopy of leaves onto that one spot than it was shining anywhere else along the channel's edge.

And so we lingered, paddles now resting across our laps, to absorb the silent scene and the fact that we were on the water with an actual wild, unrestrained crocodile. Then, noiselessly knifing our paddles through the water, we turned and headed back the way we came.

2.
Counting Crocodiles

Where we came upon the croc in the mangroves, there had been no crocodiles for many years. That lone croc was a newcomer to the area and a sign that more would soon be moving into the territory. Crocodiles are native to North America. Their original range included all of the saltwater coast of the Florida Everglades and southward via open water and mangrove channels, to the tropical hardwood hammocks and surrounding waters of Key Largo, the largest of the Florida Keys. Over time, due to hunting pressure and loss of habitat, the crocodiles dwindled in number until they were in danger of extinction. Finally protected by law, the crocodile population rebounded and steadily increased until the animals spread out of their strongholds in the Everglades and Key Largo. Today crocodiles can be found as far north as Sanibel Island on Florida's Gulf Coast, east to Biscayne Bay on the outskirts of Miami, and south all the way to Key West.

Deanna and I learned of the existence of the North American crocodile on our very first visit to the Everglades. At that time, they were still an endangered species. Only 360 were believed to be left. I wondered how the experts came up with that number and so I asked the fish and game person in charge of protecting all the crocodiles in the U.S. He told me that every so often a team of wildlife biologists would fly over the crocodile's habitat in a small plane and count all the crocs they saw. But from that high up, they couldn't see baby crocs or even crocodiles that may have been hiding in thick brush or deep dark water. So the actual number of crocodiles was higher than the official count.

Counting crocodiles sounded like fun, so Deanna and I decided to try our hand at it, not by flying over them, but by boating in the waters where we knew crocs lived. I suggested we cruise slowly in our little inflatable boat, *Leeky Teeky*. Its five-horsepower outboard was quiet, could cover a lot of backcountry water, and would take us far on a tank of gas. But Deanna refused to go looking for crocodiles in a boat that a croc might bite into and deflate, leaving us to swim in the water with the dangerous animals. We agreed to make the expedition in *Moccassin*, our twelve-foot fiberglass canoe. I named *Moccassin* with two s's because it sounds snaky like its cottonmouth namesake, and a canoe moves on the water much the way a water snake swims—silent, smooth, leaving only a trace of a wake. The canoe paddle would be quieter in the water than a motor and *Moccassin* would be a whole lot sturdier than the inflatable so Deanna would feel safer. *Moccassin* has an extra high freeboard. This is especially re-assuring when we are working in water where dangerous animals are found. Also, the canoe is the only way to go when you are carrying a lot of gear, such as video equipment, sketchpads, dive gear, and fishing tackle. The deep well of space between the fore and aft seats keeps a heavy load centered in the boat. For safety, stability, and stealth on the water, nothing beats a canoe.

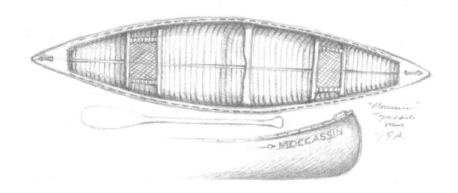

We shoved *Moccassin* into Buttonwood Canal in the Everglades National Park. We launched in front of the park's visitor center, at a spot from which a few crocodiles can always be seen sunning themselves on a large mudbank across the water. The only way to get close to those crocodiles is by boat, and people rent canoes on shore to do just that. But we wanted to explore farther into the habitat, and see crocs that were wilder and less tolerant of spectators. We hoped to find them hiding among the mangroves, and spot them diving in the deep dark water for fish, or perhaps even stalking long legged wading birds on the overgrown banks.

I did the paddling while Deanna sat forward with her camera ready. We hadn't gone very far down the canal when we spotted our first crocodile resting its huge chin up out of the water on a mangrove root. The crocodile watched us go slowly by as Deanna photographed. I estimated the croc's length at approximately eight feet. Nearly half of an alligator or crocodile's length is tail. When a crocodile or alligator is floating on the surface, its tail curves downward and out of sight. However, if you see the whole torso—head, neck, and back—you can visually estimate the torso size and double it to include the tail. When only the head is visible, as was the case of the croc resting its chin on the root, I visually estimated the length of the head which, in crocodilians, is one sixth the length of the entire body, and I did the math.

We continued down the long canal, staying a safe distance from the mangroves where we now knew large crocs could be well hidden, and we counted each one we saw. One very large crocodile, whose head was barely visible behind a tangle of roots, suddenly swam out of hiding and headed in our direction. Remembering a friend who described to me how an alligator bit the blade off his canoe paddle, I lifted my paddle up out of the water to prevent it from making any splash or swirl that might attract the already curious croc.

The crocodile passed less than ten feet from our canoe. It seemed as if it just wanted a closer look. Crocodile eyes are small but penetrating and the eye closest to us was obviously taking our measure. As the big croc swam by, parallel to our canoe, we could see its entire body, from the tip of its tapered snout to the end of its long muscular tail, waving side to side, propelling the creature powerfully through the water. The enormous beast was longer than our twelve-foot canoe!

After the monster croc had finally passed and showed no further interest in us, Deanna exhaled audibly. We both had been holding our breath. But true to her photographer's instinct, Deanna had also snapped picture after picture—some so close up that later, when I viewed them on the laptop, I could see a thin layer of dried, caked-on mud covering portions of the crocodile's head and neck.

Farther down the canal we saw something the professional crocodile counters could not see on their aerial search. We found a baby crocodile! It was only one of a clutch that had hatched from eggs their mother had buried right there on the stream bank. The others were well camouflaged in the foliage, but this one was out in the open all by itself, walking rather clumsily over pebbles and stones. I was careful not to paddle too closely knowing that the mother would be somewhere near. A breeze pushed over the water forcing me to paddle backwards to maintain a safe distance while Deanna trained her telephoto lens on our tiny prize.

We counted and photographed and videotaped and sketched crocodiles all day and returned the next day to pick up where we left off. Our count at the beginning of the second day was around twelve crocodiles and we quickly began adding to that number, counting a croc sliding in the water, another resting on a floating log, and one crawling on a long mudbank. None were bigger than the twelve footer, but a few came close in size.

A very large crocodile surprised us once when, suddenly, it opened its mouth wide to reveal the fact that it had no teeth. Not a one! A crocodile loses and replaces teeth throughout much of its life. But as a croc gets older, it gradually loses its ability to grow new teeth and, one lost tooth at a time, finally becomes toothless. Luckily for an old croc, its powerful bite is provided by huge jaw muscles, not from teeth, and a toothless croc can continue feeding with little or no change in diet. Crocodile and alligator teeth are for snagging and holding onto prey, not chewing it up. But once a croc or gator clamps its jaws tight onto an animal, the pressure alone makes escape almost impossible. All crocodilians swallow their food whole or break it up into smaller pieces to swallow whole. They do this by twisting or pounding a captured creature against a waterside tree or log. Deanna once witnessed an alligator do this in order to break apart and eat a large waterbird.

The only truly frightening experience we had counting crocodiles occurred when we came upon a ten footer dozing on a sandy shoal completely up out of the water. The crocodile's five-foot-long tail was curved into an *S* shape and pressed against the high mudbank. The wind had picked up and I was paddling hard to control the canoe. Deanna was in the bow of the boat crouching low to videotape the water ahead. The low camera angle was perfectly suited for the ten footer sleeping on the shoal and I turned the canoe to point Deanna toward her new subject.

As the canoe glided toward the bank and I began back paddling to keep Deanna from coming face to face with the sleeping crocodile, a sudden gust of wind hit us from behind, causing the canoe, and Deanna, to lurch forward. We both must have yelped loudly as the canoe sped toward the shoal, because the sleeping croc woke up, popping open both its eyes. Seeing the bow of a canoe plowing toward it, the startled crocodile leaped like an overgrown lizard, using its tail, coiled against the mudbank, as a springboard. Ten feet and four hundred pounds of crocodile launched itself off the shoal, into the air, just barely clearing the bow of our canoe, only a shiver away from Deanna, and splashed with a thunderous belly flop into the canal. Submerged and seriously spooked, it torpedoed away. Somehow Deanna managed to capture the entire experience on tape, but the near disaster on the water told us that we were getting too good at finding crocodiles in their hiding places and that, with danger imminent, it was time to bring our crocodile count to an end. In all, we counted twenty-three crocodiles. The two-day expedition in our canoe gave me a song, a picture book, a DVD about the crocodile in North America, and a great story to tell about one of our most hair-raising and unforgettable adventures afloat.

3.

Pony Island

On a warm misty coastal morning we left a sleepy little Maryland harbor and headed out to sea. Our boat was a twenty-foot open-cockpit runabout, unnamed, with a twenty-year-old 150-horsepower outboard motor that smoked and chugged and shuddered but miraculously kept running. Our captain, an amiable and experienced waterman named Greg, had borrowed the old clunker of a boat and seemed annoyed but not worried by the fitful engine. He was determined to keep it and us going for as long as it took to complete the short trip to Assateague Island, just a stone's throw from the Maryland mainland. Assateague is a 37-mile-long barrier island off the shared seacoast of Maryland and Virginia. The island is named after the Assateague Indians who, long ago, were seasonal inhabitants, camping on its shores all summer long, and living on an abundance of shellfish and crabs. Today, the island is an officially designated National Seashore and its present inhabitants are the indigenous shellfish, crabs, gulls, terns, herons, egrets, and a variety of migrating waterfowl. White-tailed deer live in the island's piney woods. Sitka deer, an Asian species introduced by man, also live there.

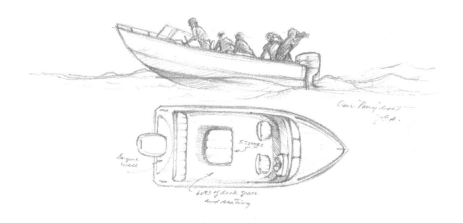

The most famous inhabitants of Assateague Island are the wild ponies. To many people, Assateague Island is the Pony Island. How the herd originally got to Assateague, no one really knows. But it is believed that the ponies, which are large and actually only a hand smaller than horses, are descended from European horses. The story is that around three hundred years ago, a ship carrying horses to the new world hit a horrendous storm and broke apart, freeing its cargo into the sea. The panicked horses kicked and swam together as a herd to the barrier island where they recovered from their ordeal and remained, feeding on the sea oats and marsh grasses. Over time, their island diet, along with inbreeding, gradually stunted the growth of each new generation of offspring, until an entirely new breed of small horse was created which has become known as the Assateague Pony.

As an artist preparing to paint the wild horses and their beautiful island home, I wanted to see the shoreline from the sea the way the shipwrecked horses may have seen it for the first time. Greg knew exactly what I was after. He himself had often beached a small boat on the island to do the same. And he would stay, watching the ponies for hours, enjoying the peace and solitude. He told me that on Assateague Island "each day is exactly the way it should be."

Later in the day we planned to drive onto the island in a jeep via the road from Chincoteague Island. Chincoteague and Assateague are sister islands, Chincoteague being the inner island—closest to the mainland—and Assateague, the out island. Neither is far offshore. Deanna and I have driven to Assateague many times on many previous visits to see and photograph the wildlife. I have videotaped big-antlered white-tailed bucks swimming in the creeks and channels, and white-tailed does with fawns only a few days old hiding in the brush. Deanna and I have watched the ponies grazing and browsing in the marshland with their foals prancing playfully nearby. And always, we have stayed past sunset when the only sounds you hear are the occasional calls of gulls or the faint splashes of pony hooves walking in the water.

Once a year the peaceful spell of Assateague Island is broken when residents of Chincoteague come for the roundup. It is a necessary intrusion. Like any wild population, the number of animals that can live in a given area is dependent on the availability of food. The long narrow strip of island can only sustain a certain number of ponies. So each year the pony loving people of Chincoteague round up the surplus, driving them to swim across the channel to the Chincoteague fairgrounds for sale. The annual pony roundup, swim, and auction has become famous. Assateague ponies are prized the world over. They are a colorful lot. Some are brown with white blotches. Others are white with brown dots. There are black and white ponies, pure white and pure black ones, grays, buckskins, and reds. All have the extra long tail and flowing mane of the wild horse.

Our boat chugged over the offshore waves and swells before finally cruising into the blue sea. Then, veering southward, captain Greg brought the boat about, and the entire length of the island came into view. Here we were, out in deep water, rising and falling with each swell. I could imagine the frightened shipwrecked horses rising and falling as they swam, struggling to keep their heads above water, while being pushed by the waves toward Assateague's long white beach. Finally, feeling bits of broken seashells tumbling around them, the exhausted horses came ashore, and folding their shivering legs on the sand, they huddled against the warm dunes and slept.

It is no longer permitted to beach a boat on Assateague Island. Our boat was too big to beach anyway, but Greg got us close enough so that we could imagine what it would be like to swim all the way to shore. As he steered off a last breaking wave and turned back toward the deep water, I spotted a small herd of ponies walking in the misty distance along the water's edge. Just then, Greg throttled up to race back to the harbor and the vision of ponies on shore faded in our spray.

That afternoon, hiking on the island, we located the band of ponies I had seen earlier from the boat. They were walking in a line on the wet beach, and occasionally wading in the surf. Crouched low on the sand, we scurried to get closer, but not too close. Wild ponies bite, kick, and will even charge. On my first visit to Assateague, I made the mistake of getting too close to a big red stallion. In an instant of fury, the animal spun on its hind legs and charged, nearly trampling me and my brand new camera equipment.

When the small herd began to move toward the dunes, we followed at a distance. They led us past the dunes to a salt marsh where we walked on firm but slippery mud, stepping on the ponies' wild unshod hoof prints. It was in the marsh where we suddenly became aware of the island's voracious mosquitoes and noticed big green horse flies buzzing around our ears and legs. To escape the hoard of biting flies, the ponies had waded right into the marsh water. By the time we reached them, they were belly deep and feeding contentedly on cord grass—a reedlike, highly nutritious marsh plant.

The still water of the marsh was a great place to watch the island's black skimmers. This large bird flies over the water with its extra long bottom bill slicing through the surface film. Skimmers catch fish this way, but the fish must be small and swimming just beneath the surface to be snapped up with such speed.

In the marsh the ponies silently waded from place to place, munching the thick-stemmed grass. As the returning tide began to flow in, the ponies began to stumble and slosh around in deepening water until they finally had to abandon the water for higher and firmer ground where they were once again vulnerable to the insatiable flies. Soon we saw long red lines of blood running down the ponies' necks and sides. Bleeding from bites, the ponies did what they could to limit the onslaught. They snorted to keep mosquitos and flies out of their noses. They shook their long manes to brush the insects away from their eyes. They swooshed their tails to swat and brush the torturous flies off their backs and hindquarters.

With no manes to shake or tails to swoosh, we batted and slapped at the flies with our hands trying to keep them away, taking care not to slap too loudly and scare the ponies away. We stayed until we could not stand the bites any longer, and left the ponies still feeding in the marsh. A little while later, we saw them back on the beach, bedding down against the protective dunes just as their kind has done for hundreds of years. And that's where we left them, as they dozed, dreaming their ancient dreams by the sea.

4.

Sunken
Treasures

Often when we head out with the intention of finding one particular thing, we discover and learn about many other things. For instance, when Deanna and I decided to learn all about rattlesnakes, we also learned about the places where they live and the habits of their prey, and we became aware of the desert tortoise with whom rattlesnakes sometimes share a burrow.

So it was, that when we headed out into the ocean for the first time in our seaworthy cruiser, *Crayfish*, to study the natural history of Florida's coral reef, we discovered something else along the way. At latitude 24.51802 N and longitude 80.40795 W, just a few miles offshore, we came upon a large yellow buoy marking the location of a rock pile clearly visible just twelve feet below. We tied *Crayfish* up to the buoy and looked around. The pile was approximately twenty feet wide, forty feet long, and five feet high. The rocks were all approximately the same size, and rounded in shape, like the boulders you see in rivers. They rested together as if they had been placed there on the sea floor, and were not part of any natural rocky outcropping.

As we peered down at the rock pile, it dawned on me what it was that we were floating over. We had happened on the remains of a shipwreck! The yellow buoy was the same type that the State of Florida uses to mark historical wrecks out in the ocean and to provide a mooring for dive boats, so divers wishing to explore will not have to drop anchor and damage the site.

Down below our boat, a brass sign identified the pile of rocks as all that remains of the San Pedro, a Spanish galleon that sunk on that spot over two hundred years ago. The rounded rocks had been gathered from a river in Spain and used as ballast, carefully placed in the bottom of the tall ship to provide a counterweight to the mast and sails. Smooth rounded river rocks would not cut into the wooden hull the way jagged sea rocks would. For us, finding the wreck was like discovering a portal to history out in the ocean, and we happily sailed through, eager to learn more.

In 1733 a fleet of twenty-three Spanish galleons sailing from South America to Spain entered the Florida Strait, a ninety-mile-wide strip of the Atlantic Ocean that lies between Cuba and the Florida Keys. A galleon is a wooden vessel with a wide and roomy hull for carrying tons of cargo, armed with heavy cannons to protect against pirates or any other warships that might try to overtake them.

The 1733 fleet was particularly concerned about pirates because they were all carrying treasure, including tons of silver bars, silver and gold coins, gold ingots, large emeralds and other precious gems. The ships sailed in a long line forming a kind of wagon train that could quickly circle and become a large fighting force if attacked. But it wasn't pirates or warships that hit the armada as it passed through the straits. It was a powerful storm with hurricane-force winds and mammoth waves that drove the treasure-laden ships aground in shallow water, broke them up, sunk them to the bottom, and scattered their valuable cargo across the sea floor.

The entire fleet went down in the order they had been traveling, and lay on the bottom in less than twenty feet of water. Immediately after the hurricane, the Spanish government attempted to salvage the treasure only to be thwarted by sharks, now in a feeding frenzy because of the many drownings caused by the hurricane. The salvage effort was abandoned, and the fleet was left where it lay. The ships' timbers slowly rotted. The cannons and anchors rusted. And the treasure gradually became covered and hidden by layers of sand.

In the 1950s and '60s modern treasure hunters located the rock piles, determined they were ships' ballast piles, and one by one began uncovering the remains of the long sunken fleet. Most of their work was done near shore in sight of land. Soon, their discoveries became widely known, and U.S. Highway 1, which parallels the shoreline in plain sight of those waters, was dubbed Galleon Alley.

The San Pedro wreck site alone yielded cannons, anchors, coins, jewelry, precious stones, pewter pots, and many other historic artifacts. Today the San Pedro wreck site is a public preserve. You can visit it online at http://bit.ly/waterstories-sanpedro.

The web site shows divers exploring the ballast rock pile, surrounded by marine life. The pile is also a favorite place for hungry sharks, attracted to the many species of fish living amid the rocks, now encrusted with barnacles and grown thick with sponges and coral. We have seen six-foot-long blacktip and lemon sharks, eight-foot-long nurse sharks, and twelve-foot-long hammerheads swimming in this water. Bull and tiger sharks also cruise the area.

I found out what digging in the bottom was like for the treasure hunters when I anchored *Crayfish* in a shallower spot nearby and snorkeled around.

Deanna stayed on board and nervously watched for sharks while I was down. The sea floor was made up of loose sand and bits of coral crushed to a powder by the pounding action of the waves. The sand and coral powder bottom is held in place and stabilized by the roots of seagrass which grows in large patches. But between the patches of seagrass, the bottom is extremely soft, and I could dig my fingers deep into it. Because of the way the treasure ships were broken up by the waves, much of their cargo was broadcast over a wide area. It was possible that, even where I was snorkeling, I might scoop out a silver coin or piece of gold chain.

Every small fish or ray that dashed away from me created a large cloud of loosened sand and coral powder in the water. Such soft loose bottom had more than two hundred years to cover the sunken treasure of the lost 1733 fleet. The only way the treasure hunters recovered it was by blowing the powdery sand away using a long air hose and sifting through the layers of heavier sand beneath with rakes or their bare hands. When something was found it was carried above to be examined carefully to see what it might be. Two hundred years is a long time. Sunken objects become unrecognizable. Silver bars and ingots turn black and can look like plain old rocks. Precious gems are encrusted with minerals. Only gold still shines. But a treasure hunter knows what to look for. Every treasure hunter I have met has been a seaman, mapmaker, diver, scientist, metallurgist, and historian all rolled into one.

When I emerged from my dive, Deanna reminded me that the treasure we had come to Florida to find was the natural treasure of the coral reef. In particular, Alligator Reef, named after the USS *Alligator*, a naval schooner that hit the reef and broke into pieces in 1822. Today Alligator Reef is marked by a lighthouse to warn mariners of the jagged danger just beneath the surface.

Getting to Alligator Reef in our small boat was high adventure. Crossing a wide channel where gigantic commercial ships and freighters plow the water creating waves five and six feet high, I felt like a mouse trying to cross a busy superhighway. *Crayfish* was tossed around like a cork in the wakes of the big ships. But we didn't sink, and the rewards for braving the passage were great.

Alligator Reef is the highest crest of a massive underwater shelf that includes the shoreline beach. The whole shelf is comprised of: the crushed coral shoreline; the sand flats, where the water is one to six feet deep; a trough naturally dug out by the rolling action of incoming waves; a deeper channel created by ship traffic; an upward sloping back reef culminating in the jagged reef crest; and finally, the steep drop off the continental shelf, where the water depth plunges hundreds of feet.

We lingered on the back reef, where we could see the bottom through the clean shallow water as clearly as if we had been snorkeling. *Crayfish*'s two-foot draft (the part of the boat under water) kept us floating safely above the fan coral, brain coral, elkhorn coral, and the many different types of sponges growing on the slope.

We watched small fish swimming over isolated mounds of coral called patch reefs. Fishing near one of these patches, I caught a hefty, butter-colored Nassau grouper and a long trumpet fish, both of which Deanna photographed up close before I let them go.

Out on the reef crest, spaced a few hundred feet apart, were more official-looking yellow buoys like the one over the San Pedro. These also provided holding for boats without their having to be anchored. Anchors can damage coral, and damaged coral will die or take a very long time to recover. We found Alligator Reef to be home to the goliath grouper. Goliath grouper can grow to be six feet long and weigh over four hundred pounds. Big nurse sharks and huge stingrays cruise back and forth over the colorful coral, then suddenly settle down on the sandy bottom to wait and ambush passing fish, crabs, and lobsters. And just beyond the reef, where the bottom drops deep, sailfish patrol the ledges, searching for schools of mackerel that they can slash through with their long sharp bills, cutting and stunning the fish before gobbling them down.

After an afternoon slowly drifting over the corals and sponges and schools of colorful fish, I started the engine to head home. Our trip back to the shore was calm with no big ships passing by. No huge wakes to negotiate. As I steered into the marked channel that led to our dock, I was thinking treasure: the living treasure of the coral reef and the sunken treasure of the ancient shipwrecks. It was easy to imagine that beautiful yellow grouper I had caught and released swimming around a sunken chest brimming with silver coins yet to be discovered.

5.

Super

Moon Sharks

I was working on a series of paintings of saltwater fish. Before I started each new picture, I went fishing in the ocean, and on more than a few occasions, I'd catch the very species of fish I had planned to paint. Deanna photographed these fish up close for me before I let them go. I made sure to write down observations of the ocean habitat where they lived. We'd also drive twice a day—at noon and 4:30 p.m.—to see what the offshore fishing boats had brought in. There I sketched and Deanna photographed freshly caught tuna, mackerel, wahoo, and dorado. When it came to painting tarpon, barracuda, and sharks, I had plenty of potential subjects that were cruising in the waters around the local docks. But to catch and photograph a really big tarpon or shark, I knew I had to go out at night when they go on the prowl and hunt for food.

Fishing in the dark is not for everybody. Boating at night can be tricky, especially in the shallow waters of the Florida Keys where navigation is done primarily by water color—"Green or blue, sail on through; if it's brown, go around." At night the water is not green or blue, or brown. It is uniformly black. I hired a guide who was experienced both in navigating at night and fishing for large dangerous fish in the dark. One cool clear evening, just before sunset, I found myself heading out to sea to fish for tarpon and sharks with a fishing friend named Rick, and our guide, Captain Bill. Deanna opted to stay home. Nothing about this adventure appealed to her.

Captain Bill's boat was designed for fishing the water near the shore, where the bottom is flat and the crystal clear water only a foot deep in places. Flats boats, as they are called, are approximately eighteen feet long, and very light, drawing only three or four inches of water. That means with the outboard motor tilted up out of the water, a flats boat can float in even less than a foot of water, clearing submerged sandbars and drifting safely over ecologically fragile seagrass beds. To move across such shallow fishing grounds, the fishing guide stands up on a high platform and pushes the boat using a long pole. Done right, poling is nearly soundless and the very

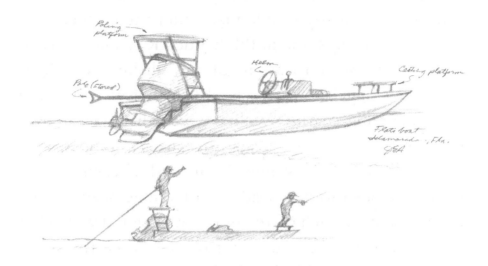

best way to sneak up on ultra wary shallow-water species such as bonefish and permit.

In deeper water, with its ninety-horsepower motor down, a flats boat skims across the surface at forty-five miles per hour. That's how fast Captain Bill was going as we headed out into the sunset to catch big fish. His face was covered with a blue bandana to protect his skin from the wind. The bandana mask and sunglassed eyes made him look like a modern day pirate. Rick turned his red Ohio State ball cap around and stared squarely into the wind. I held my long billed fishing hat in my lap and squinted my eyes to protect them from the sea spray hitting my face as we raced over green water into blue, and finally came to rest at the edge of a large brown patch of water, where a sandbar was clearly visible just under the surface.

Immediately Captain Bill handed Rick and me each a rod baited with a tiny bit of raw shrimp. The light rods were rigged to catch small fish that we could use as bait for big sharks. While we were fishing for bait, Captain Bill rigged two heavy rods, each equipped with a reel full of 60 lb. test line. At the end of each line, he twisted on a short wire leader with a huge heavy-gauge hook attached. Each of the hooks was baited with a big chunk of fish; one with a cut of mackerel, the other with a long filet of jack. The lines with heavily baited hooks were each lobbed out into the water and the rods secured in the boat's forward rod holders.

I held out my hand and aligned my fingers with the horizon, using a seaman's method of measuring the time until sunset—five minutes for each finger. The sun was about three fingers, or fifteen minutes away from the horizon when the first big rod was suddenly jerked down and Rick was onto a heavy fish. Tarpon? Shark? We couldn't see. But after a few minutes of the fish tugging and hugging the bottom, Captain Bill said, "That's a shark. A tarpon would have leaped high out of the water by now." Rick fought the fish for about five minutes before finally reeling it up to the surface, when we saw that it was a blacktip shark, about four feet long and weighing approximately forty pounds. By the time Rick got the shark beside the boat where I could photograph it, the sun was almost down. As Captain Bill was unhooking the shark, I took note of its pointed white teeth, large black eyes, and the tiny black ampullae on its snout, which are pores in the skin that can sense electrical impulses of fleeing prey, and help the shark locate food even in total darkness.

Captain Bill quickly released the shark. Then he reeled in all lines, and we moved on, speeding through a long straight ditch that cut through the mangroves. The sky was darkening but the water remained bright and colorful. At twilight water has a way of holding daylight, even as the sky dims. Captain Bill steered out of the ditch and tore across a small bay before finally slowing down to cruise quietly, almost reverently, by a large section of wooded shoreline. In the woods the roof of a house could be seen.

"That's where Johnny Weissmuller lived." Bill said, staring at the hidden house. Something in his voice gave the impression that he was reliving some past happiness.

Johnny Weissmuller was a world record–holding swimmer. Back in the 1930's, he won three gold medals in the Olympics. Later he embarked on a motion picture career and starred in a series of Tarzan movies playing the jungle hero and creating the famous call still recognized today as the "Tarzan Yell." When Captain Bill was a boy his family lived close by, just across the canal from his childhood hero. "I remember laying in bed at night and hearing the lions roar," he told us. The "movie Tarzan" had real lions for pets.

We picked up speed and raced nightfall to the Channel Two Bridge, site of many great battles between fishermen and really big fish. I was still thinking about the lions as we neared the cement arches of the old bridge. Then my thoughts quickly shifted back to big fish as Captain Bill dropped anchor and began letting out all of his hundred or so feet of anchor line. He had taken his sunglasses off and without them he looked like an entirely different person. His eyes were small and much closer together than I had imagined when they were covered by the dark lenses.

He was smiling and humming softly as he attached a small buoy to keep the last five feet of anchor line afloat, then tied the very end of the line to the stern of his boat. The water was pitch black. The big rods were cast. And in the fading light of day we waited for a bite.

A tarpon is a large silver fish of the western Atlantic Ocean with a wide square jaw that drops open like the door of a cargo plane, and snaps closed with an audible pop. Tarpon grow to be six feet long and weigh up to 250 pounds. Of all the silver-sided fish in the sea, tarpon shine the brightest and leap the highest. I wanted very much to hook into one to see it leap, and I sat staring at the rod tips wishfully thinking "tarpon, tarpon," attempting to will one to our bait. I heard Captain Bill whispering, "tarpon … C'mon." All three of us were lost in anticipation.

Big fish began rolling up to the surface, less than fifty feet off our bow. Then others surfaced between us and the bridge. All of the rolling backs showed the long spearlike ray of a tarpon dorsal fin. Captain Bill was whispering more loudly "take the bait . . . take it," when one of the rods jerked down violently. And it was my turn to take it!

Moonlight beginning to shine through the arched aqueduct of the old bridge illuminated my line as it cut through the surface, straining under the weight of a heavy fish. I pressed the butt of the rod into my stomach and hauled back, reeling in line whenever there was a pause in the fish's powerful pull. It stayed deep, the way Rick's blacktip shark did. When the fight finally came to the surface, I reeled as hard as I could and dragged another shark up against the side of the boat. This one was a four-foot lemon shark, a bit thicker and heavier than the blacktip.

The lemon's struggling against my line must have worked as an attractant because as soon as we had released my shark, Rick began reeling in another. Rick's fish pulled so strongly it began dragging the boat, pulling hard on the anchor. Captain Bill quickly untied the anchor line and threw it in the water where the buoy kept the rope afloat. Releasing us from the anchor allowed Rick's big fish to pull the free-floating boat across the water. This fish was a monster! It towed the eighteen-foot boat steadily through the blackness, and the white moonlit trail on the surface behind the boat showed us just how far.

To further reduce the pressure on Rick's straining rod, the captain started the engine and motored slowly, following the course of the pulling fish. Even so, reeling in the fish didn't come easy. With his broad back bent over and his arms tensed against the powerful tug of the fish, Rick worked hard for every yard of retrieved line.

The fish finally came up splashing and thrashing on the surface, and we couldn't believe our eyes. It was a gigantic nurse shark, more than eight feet long from tail tip to snout! The head was two feet wide. Captain Bill guessed the shark's weight at around 125 pounds. I snapped what photos I could in the dark. Then Captain Bill reached down, removed the hook with a quick turn, and the big bruiser of a shark slowly sank and swam away.

The tarpon were still rolling on the surface but we couldn't see them. We only heard their splashes in the dark and they didn't seem to be interested in what we were offering. The moon climbed higher, full and brilliant in the indigo sky. It looked much bigger than usual. It looked supersized. We learned later that it was in fact a Super Moon—the moon was actually closer to the Earth than usual. The last time it had come as close was eighteen years ago, and it will be eighteen more years before it comes as close again. Compared to the gigantic white ball in the night sky everything looked dwarfed—the bridge; the silhouetted mangrove islands; even the sea, shimmering in reflected moonlight.

We cast our lines in the glow of the big moon, but even the fish must have fallen under its spell, because the rods did not move. Rick was done in. I was satisfied.

Captain Bill was smiling. He started the engine, flipped on the red, green, and white running lights, and slowly, triumphantly headed his lovely little boat home.

6.

Our Very Own Lake Monster

Lake Champlain lies between northeastern New York State and northwestern Vermont, and reaches northward into Canada. The lake is a hundred miles long and twenty-five miles wide at its northern end, which includes the Champlain Islands and a portion of the lake called the Inland Sea. The deepest part of this enormous freshwater lake is at the narrow southern end where the dark, cold bottom is four hundred feet down.

The average depth of the lake is sixty-four feet. Much of Lake Champlain's five hundred mile shoreline is undeveloped and remains just the way it must have looked when the French explorer Samuel de Champlain first canoed down the lake over four hundred years ago.

For us, Lake Champlain is a second home where we fish and swim and where my boat *Crayfish* summers on its mooring. From Crinkle Cove on North Hero Island we can look westward across a wide shallow bay and see the distant inlet that leads to the broader, deeper water of the lake. Sometimes I sit in the big chair on shore and watch sunlight sparkling on the waves, while my mind wanders into wonder. I wonder about the shape of the lake bottom, where the rocks and weeds are, and how many sunken boats are preserved by the coldest water down deep. I wonder about the fish and eels and turtles swimming beneath the surface. And I wonder about Champ, the lake's legendary monster.

Lake Champlain is one of a group of deep, cold-water lakes which includes Loch Ness in Scotland and Cadbury Lake in Canada, that lay within the ring in the northern part of the globe known as the "Monster Latitudes." Of all the world's lakes, those in the northern latitudes have had the most reports of mysterious animals inhabiting their waters. The record of monster sightings in Lake Champlain dates back as early as Samuel de Champlain's own report of seeing a long serpentine animal as big around as a barrel. And before de Champlain, the Indians native to the area told stores of a gigantic snake living in the water.

The most recent sightings of the unknown creature in Lake Champlain describe either a twenty-five-foot-long, dark colored animal with a long slender neck and a head like a large anaconda or a similarly long and dark creature with a short thick neck and horse-like head. The two persistent descriptions suggest that a couple of different undiscovered species are being seen. This fits with the history of most sea monster sightings which seem to be evenly divided between sightings of a "water horse" and sightings of a long necked plesiosaur-like creature. Deanna and I have spotted an unidentified animal in the lake that could have been either. Whatever people are seeing, those of us who live on the lake's shore and boat on its cool blue water, feel privileged to have such marvelous and mysterious neighbors to ponder and watch for. There are times when we actually go out on the water specifically to look for "Champ," the name used by locals for any of Lake Champlain's shadowy creatures. But most of our time on the lake is spent studying the known life in the water.

To learn more about the deep-water plants and fish and the topography of the lake, I installed a small underwater TV camera. It has a fifty-foot cable with an infrared video camera to let it see in the dark. A small TV screen on the deck allows us to view what the camera captures below.

Crayfish is the perfect boat for exploring. Its compact nineteen-foot length makes it easy for one person to handle. And its wide beam (the width from side to side) makes for a very stable ride in all types of conditions. *Crayfish* has a deep V-shaped hull to plow smoothly through waves and a shallow enough draft to explore weedy coves. With the big 130-horsepower outboard motor tilted up, I can cruise safely in less than two feet of depth.

There's a cabin to store fishing rods and tackle and camera gear and sketching supplies; a pilot house for shelter from sun or rain; and a canvas door to close out cold weather. The large open deck has plenty of space for photography or handling big fish.

The boat's GPS (Global Positioning Satellite) tells me where I am and maps a dotted trail home if I get caught out in the fog or after dark. A sonar screen shows the depth of the water and fish shapes, and also outlines the bottom contour. The underwater TV gives an actual picture of the world beneath the waves. And the VHF radio is my lifeline to shore, and help, in case of an emergency.

Most of the time Deanna and I go out on the boat together. Sometimes I go out alone. I was alone one day, exploring an underwater ledge by slowly towing the submerged TV camera on its long cable. At the base of the rock ledge where the lake bottom was flat, I discovered a bed of freshwater mussels similar to the native species of large mussel we often find near shore. The longer I drifted over the flat bottom, the more mussels I saw, and the more crowded were the clusters of mussels on the sea floor, twenty-five feet down.

I wondered if it was just that one spot where mussels flourished. So, I moved a few miles down the lake and

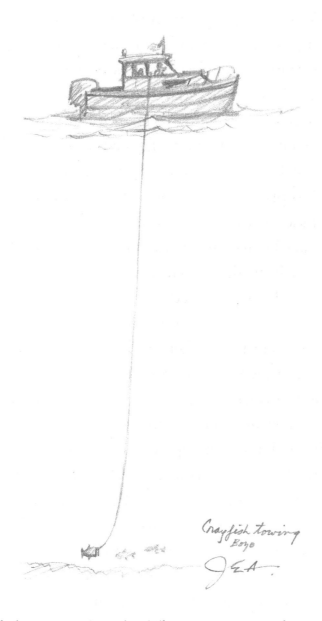

Crayfish towing
Boyo
JEA

lowered the camera again. There too, mussels covered the lake bottom. There were acres and acres of mussels. The mussels were crammed so closely together, I saw no sandy spots between them. Freshwater mussels are good food for wildlife. Otters and raccoons often feast on mussels found along the shore. And down deep, sturgeon, catfish, and drum crunch on mussel shells to eat the succulent mollusks inside. I wondered if the millions, maybe billions of freshwater mussels living in lake Champlain could also be a food source for Champ. Indeed, a whole colony of Champ animals might be able to survive on such an abundant food supply. I began planning an expedition that would include my three grandsons and Deanna as crew, to search the lake bottom for more mussels plus edible weeds, and forage fish, in those places where numerous Champ sightings have been reported.

We cast off on a sunny morning with great expectations for a good time together on the water. Neither myself, Deanna, Darren, who was fourteen at the time, Derek, who was ten, nor Conner, six, actually expected to find Champ. Champ sightings are rarely sought. They are chance happenings. But if we did see Champ, we were ready with video and still cameras. Our plan was to look at as much water as we could—surface and below—using the TV camera, and write down what we saw at ten feet, twenty feet, thirty feet, all the way down to fifty feet, the maximum depth our underwater video cable could reach. Through surface surveillance, we'd make a note of any logs, sticks, waterbirds, swimming dogs, and mysterious waves that could be mistaken for a monster in the water. And lastly, we would occasionally scan the perimeter of the lake with binoculars just in case Champ popped up to see what we were doing.

Each of us had a job to do. I operated the boat. Darren was in charge of the underwater camera, which the boys had named "Bozo." He lowered it for us to see the lake bottom on the TV screen, and raised it whenever it drifted into an obstacle or when we were moving to a new location.

Wherever we lowered Bozo we found mussels. In every case they were mostly the large common freshwater mussels, with a mingling of a smaller species called zebra mussels because of their striped shells. Mussels are filter feeders, filtering the water to strain out microscopic organisms. For there to be so many mussels carpeting acres of lake bottom, there has to be enough microscopic food to feed them. Some scientists worry that the invasive zebra mussels, whose larvae have been carried in on the feet of birds and the hulls of boats, will eventually alter the nature of the lake. But the larger species of mussels have been filtering the lake water for a long time with no ill effect, and have become numerous enough to be an abundant source of food for various species of native aquatic animals.

In fifty feet of water Bozo showed us a bottom of mostly rocks and sand with deep-water weeds, but no mussels. Finding weeds in water that deep and dark was surprising. Down deep we also were surprised by the presence of massive schools of white perch, a fish we rarely catch with rod and reel.

In one shallow weedy cove, Derek and Conner got out of the boat and took turns snorkeling around with the video camera, encased in its waterproof housing. Both boys captured great scenes of bright weedy shallows with sunfish and bass swimming by the camera lens. Later we looked at their footage and wrote down all the different weeds we saw, from towering columns of milfoil to tangled clumps of water cabbage to long strands of eelgrass and coontail. All of this submerged vegetation, along with the emergent aquatic plants such as cattails, reeds, water lilies, and pickerelweed, provide food and cover for Lake Champlain's warm-water species of fish, as well as habitat for amphibians, turtles, snails, crustaceans, and aquatic insects. All of which are themselves a rich food source for ducks, geese, muskrats and diving birds.

After searching for four days, our conclusion was that there was enough food in Lake Champlain to easily support animals the size of alligators or crocodiles—animals with similar body bulk as the unknown creatures people have reported seeing. A whole colony of "Champ" animals could live in the lake. And even though we didn't see any lake monsters, we did learn just how vast and rich and dark and mysterious the lake was. What we see on the surface is just that—the surface. And we learned that to really get to know any body of water, you have to look beneath the surface.

I saved one lake location for last—latitude 44.47649 N, longitude 73.19427 W—a very special place, miles from shore, where the bottom drops steeply from thirty-five feet to over one hundred feet. It was in this spot where, one spring day, Deanna and I actually saw Champ swimming less than two hundred feet away from our boat. The water was so calm, it was flat and mirror-like, perfectly reflecting the distant Adirondack Mountains of New York. I was going slowly, watching ahead for any tree trunks, branches, or other debris that had been trapped in the winter ice and would now be floating in the cold water. Deanna remarked that it was the kind of day—windless and calm—that people see Champ.

Just then, dead ahead, I saw what I thought was a long log suddenly pop up to the surface. I throttled down to slow the boat and steered to pass the obstruction on my starboard side. Keeping a safe distance away, I shifted to neutral and let *Crayfish* idle while Deanna and I walked out on deck to look at the thing in the water.

Before our eyes, the object rose about six inches higher revealing a long black shape that tapered to a point at one end. The other end, approximately twenty-five feet from the tapered end, was blunt, rounded, and lighter in color. It didn't look at all like the wooden stump of a log. It looked like a head with wet gray hair. All I could think of was how a seal's fur looks shiny and smooth when it is wet. Little by little the head, which was about the size of a soccer ball, rose until it was much higher out of the water than the rest of the twenty-five-foot length. I was speechless, completely mesmerized by the sight. Then Deanna said, "Look, it's moving!"

The tail end swayed side to side, the way a muskrat's tail does when floating on the surface. Then the entire mass began moving forward, creating a V-shaped wake in the water.

"Holy smokes!" I said to myself as we watched what both of us realized was a large animal that could only be the creature people called Champ! It was awesome. There was a video camera in the boat but it never occurred to us to get it and record the phenomenon. All we could do was stare.

The animal, whose head, neck, backbone, and tail was all that we could see on the surface, swam forward for about six feet before submerging tail first, then its back, then its head, the way I've often seen turtles submerge. And once completely submerged, it left an oval "footprint" or vacancy ring on the calm surface, just the way all large swimming animals do when they go under.

I suddenly snapped out of the spell of the remarkable sighting and ran to shift the engine into gear so we could cruise over the spot where the creature went down. A wind was picking up and the water surface was quickly changing from flat calm to choppy. By the time I was motoring over the place where the animal had submerged, the wind had gotten downright mean. The waves were closely spaced and three feet high. On the sonar screen a large dark shape showed briefly. It could have been the creature. It could have been a school of perch. It didn't really matter. We saw what we saw.

Whitecaps frothed on the crests of the oncoming waves and I had a time of it just getting *Crayfish* headed into the breakers. Our little boat bounced like a bobber on the angry seas. We had a long, rough ride home, but all the way, in my mind's eye, I could still see Champ, not mythical or magical, but natural and real, floating silently with its long tapered tail slowly sculling side to side in the calm.

7.

Ducking Puffins
and
Surfing with Seals

There is a right boat for every purpose. When I wanted to learn the basic elements of seamanship—water, wind, and weather—I took up sailing, the most basic of all methods of boating. I named my sailboat Mayfly because its single mast and mainsail reminded me of the upright wings of a mayfly floating on the water. I sailed Mayfly in calm weather and in thirty-mile-an-hour winds with waves and swells five feet high. I learned a lot about boating while sailing that boat, such as how to keep the water from getting in when the seas were rough and how to keep myself from falling out when the boat was rocked wildly by another boat's wake or heeled over on its side in a stiff breeze. I learned how to use a headwind as a brake when approaching a dock or mooring, and how to set an anchor so that it held bottom. I learned about the raw power of air and water. I felt them as the wind filled the sails and the current pressed strongly against the rudder. And I learned to respect but not fear the waves when they lifted the boat or came splashing over the bow.

I also learned that sailing was not for me. I wanted to get places faster and more directly than the wind allowed. I wanted to move quickly even on a windless day and be able to race back to shore whenever a storm threatened. I sailed Mayfly for the very last time on a cold November day, bringing the boat in to the marina to be hauled out for the winter. Snow was falling. Big flakes landed on my coat, the deck, and the water. Lake Champlain's salmon, which only come into the bays in late fall and early spring, were rising to the dimples on the water created by the falling snow. With the mainsail starboard, I ran with the frigid wind to my final port of call as a sailor.

I truly became a boatman under power, gradually increasing engine size from four horsepower to 5, 25,

75, and 130 horsepower. By motoring to a destination, I could concentrate more fully on my surroundings rather than on the boat and the business of sailing. Under power, the motor does the work. All you have to do is adjust the throttle to increase or decrease speed, and steer. But even among motorboats there is a right boat for every task.

When Deanna and I wanted to photograph and videotape the puffins that breed on an island off the coast of Maine, the best boat for the voyage turned out to be a sixty-five-year-old fishing trawler named the *Laura B.*

At forty-eight feet it was long enough to handle the offshore waves and deep troughs between them. And its narrow deck made it possible to see the ocean on both sides of the boat without having to move from rail to rail in order to keep a lookout for the tiny seabirds we were seeking. The deck was large enough to accommodate a dozen or so passengers; the captain, crew, and one amiable yellow Labrador that spent most of his time collecting soft-spoken words and gentle pats from the strangers on board.

We sailed out of the harbor in Port Clyde, Maine, for Puffin Island, which was one of an offshore chain known as the St. George Islands. Before we headed out to sea, the captain stopped to check a few lobster traps. The first trap he hauled up was empty. The second had two lobsters inside, one male and one female, as we learned when a crewmember held the lobsters up to show us their undersides. Every lobster has feelers underneath where the tail meets the carapace. The feelers of male lobsters are long; the females' feelers are short.

In another trap, there was a tiny lobster the size of a freshwater crayfish. This lobster had to be released of course, but it was a full-fledged lobster nonetheless. Lobsters begin life in the egg, hatch as larvae, and quickly develop into completely formed lobsters by the time they are a half-inch in length.

After all the traps had been emptied, re-baited with salted fish, and lowered back down, we headed seaward for the St. George Islands, which lie ten miles offshore at the outer edges of Muscongus Bay. This cluster of islands includes large inhabited islands such as Monhegan Island, and smaller wild islands where seabirds and seals find refuge from the waves. The *Laura B.* was taking us to a tiny rock of an island called Puffin Island because the small parrot-like birds nest on it each year. On our way, we passed many other rocky outcroppings, most of which had seals lounging on them. Waves splashed up and over the sprawling masses of animals. Very few seals were in the water. It must have been some sort of seal siesta.

As the *Laura B.* cruised by the bunches of lazy looking seals, I recalled another time off the coast of Maine when Deanna and I hired a Casco Bay captain and his very small boat to take us out to videotape seals. The boat, a sixteen-foot cruiser named *Sea Escape*, could handle the more predictable waves in the deep open sea. But I wondered how it would do around the rocks where the seals were and the sea splashed white with foam.

Leaving the boating to the captain, I set up my tripod and camera on the deck and waited to tape the seals as soon as we saw them. We found them all gathered on two large rocks, with quite a few seals in the water swimming around the rocks. The little boat bounced and rocked so wildly, I couldn't keep any of the animals in frame. Frothy waves splashed high into the boat, making the deck very slippery. Deanna tried to help me by holding the tripod steady, but it wasn't the tripod that was moving and blurring the video. It was the boat. I removed the tripod and held the heavy camera on my shoulder, thinking that by bending and flexing my legs I could compensate for the boat's wild movement.

Our captain, Les, saw me struggling to steady myself and made an effort to help by steering in closer and closer to the rocks, surfing his boat in the foam where the seals were also surfing. Sea Escape slid over the worst of the breakers, glided right into the foam with the frolicking seals, and stayed just long enough to allow me to get some good footage before getting into danger of running aground.

Les knew just how far he could safely approach the rocks before he had to veer off and power out. He did this again and again, surfing his little boat close to the seals and turning back out until I had gotten all the seals on tape—the ones on the rocks and those surfing in the foam. All thanks to Captain Les and *Sea Escape*.

The seals lounging on the rocks in Muscongus Bay were just the opposite of the surfing seals of Casco Bay. The *Laura B.* slowly cruised by the motionless animals, close enough for Deanna to take some excellent, rock steady photos. The animals were a mix of large

gray seals and smaller brown harbor seals. They all lay
draped over one another like piles of puppies in a ken-
nel; some yawning, some stretching, some slowly rais-
ing a flipper in the bright warm sunlight.

We could see far in the distance and count the islands
small and large that form the St. George chain. Suddenly,
a small black bird flew across our bow. The ship's mate
called it a guillemot. Guillemots are in the same family as
puffins, which also includes auks and murres—all small
black seabirds with powerful legs for swimming and diving and sharp pointed wings designed for speed of flight.
Soon more guillemots flew by the boat, along with a few
puffins. Their bright orange, parrot-like bills stood out,
even in rapid flight. The birds sped by, flying parallel to
the boat. Some zoomed over the boat, causing the people
on board to duck out of the way.

The puffins and guillemots sped over the water so closely together and so near the waves, I watched with my binoculars to see if any wing tips touched other wing tips or skimmed the tops of the waves. None did. They flew in highly coordinated, seemingly telepathic formations, turning together, rising together. Deanna was running all over the deck trying to photograph the birds speeding by. I had a better time of it using video. I could follow a bird all during its flight, rather than try to snatch a momentary still picture. The birds flew this way all the time. There was no slowing down. Whenever a bird saw something in the water to eat, it would instantly drop out of the air as if shot by a gun, and a second later emerge speeding away with a silver-sided fish.

In the midst of all the frenetic activity of the birds darting around us, the *Laura B.* suddenly slowed way down and eased alongside a round lump of an island about the size of a football field. The captain kept the big boat in place with his controls while his passengers all moved to the port side to see puffins standing still at last on the rocks and grass and ledges near the waves. Guillemots nest in crevices between or under rocks, and they can breed on islands comprised of rock alone. But puffins breed only on islands where there is enough soil for them to dig their burrow nests. A pair of puffins will dig a tunnel two feet deep and at the end of the tunnel, nestled in a bed of dry grass and downy breast feathers, a single white egg is laid. This

Guillemot

Puffin

rock dome of an island had the soil and also the height needed for puffins to nest down in their earthen tunnels while still being well above the pounding waves.

From the deck of the *Laura B.*, we could see puffins standing near their tunnels, and some birds emerging from their tunnels. There were also puffins flying in and landing on the grassy island with multiple fish clasped in their beaks, the silver fish all hanging down in a row like clothes on a line. Deanna squeezed under the ship's rail to get as close as possible to the water and the island. She even took her shoes off to hang her bare feet over the side and shoot from a sitting position. Besides puffins, she also had some colorful eider ducks to photograph; and in the air, a multitude of gulls.

The puffins walked upright like penguins do, and when one dived into the water, it walked to the edge of a tiny cliff and simply dropped off head first. There was no slow, graceful motion in anything I saw them do. They were unlike any other waterbird I had seen. When the boat came too close to one bird on a rock, the puffin simply slid off and splashed clumsily into the water, exactly the way a turtle slides off a floating log.

Throughout all this activity, the ship's dog lay near the pilothouse, dozing. All the attention he had gotten on the way out was now being showered on the birds. Even the crew had been lost to the dizzying little creatures. The captain told us that the longest returnee to the breeding island had been flying back every year for twenty-eight years. And as far as he knew, the eldest puffin on the island was thirty-six years old. Before hearing that I don't think I ever even considered the age of birds. "Wow," I wondered, "how long does a bluebird, owl, or heron live?"

The afternoon went by quickly. When we suddenly heard the engine get louder, we knew the boat was pulling away from the island. It was time to leave. The *Laura B.* cruised into Port Clyde just in the nick of time. My stomach was beginning to growl. Deanna and I both were getting hungry and looking forward to dinner by the sea. The old dog was up, standing on deck granting each disembarking passenger one last pat on his sunny yellow head. His tail was wagging. He also knew dinnertime was near.

8.

The Gulf Stream

When we explored the coral reef, we ended up learning about the entire reef system, from the beach, to the seagrass flats, to the deep trough, to the gradually inclining slope of the back reef, and finally the reef crest itself.

Beyond the reef the bottom dropped steeply to the open sea. And though there is a sameness to waves and deep water where any bottom features are out of sight many fathoms below, there are characteristics that set some of the sea's water apart from that of the surrounding ocean. These are the currents that flow north, south, east, or west. In the Atlantic Ocean there is one current so large and powerful that it can be seen and felt for thousands of miles. This current is known as the Gulf Stream.

The Gulf Stream originates in the tropical waters of the Caribbean Sea and the subtropical Gulf of Mexico. Warm Caribbean water flowing northward mixing with the warm water flowing south and east out of the Gulf forms a single tremendous torrent of warm water rushing northward toward the upper Atlantic.

As the massive flow of an estimated 2,500 million cubic feet of water squeezes between Florida and Cuba, the current picks up speed. Traveling swiftly, this great Gulf Stream, fifty miles wide, 2,100 feet deep, with a tropical 77 °F surface temperature, is a rich feeding ground for many of the ocean's largest predators. Sharks, swordfish, and marlin hunt the multitudes of smaller fish drawn into the overpowering current.

The sheer volume of oily fish such as mackerel and small tunas being killed, chomped, and cut to pieces by bigger fish, combined with the naturally greater saltiness of warm tropical water, creates a physical difference in the consistency of the water and a color that is a much darker blue in the Gulf Stream than it is in the surrounding sea. This is the deep dark water where Santiago, Ernest Hemingway's fisherman in the story *The Old Man and The Sea*, catches a giant marlin only to have it torn to shreds by the Gulf Stream's mako sharks.

The first time I saw the Gulf Stream I was so strongly moved by the sight, I felt as if all of the volume of its inky blue-black water had washed over me. We had been sailing in the cobalt blue water just offshore, deep sea fishing about four miles beyond the reef. The boat was a thirty-seven-foot offshore fishing boat named *Sea Smoke*, fresh from its trip south from Massachusetts to spend the winter in the tropics. *Sea Smoke* is a big old-style offshore fishing vessel. The big diesel engine is down below decks, leaving the stern wide open for hauling huge fish over the transom. These boats have two and sometimes three levels. The captain steers from either the second or third level, to scan the distant water for schools of bluefish or tuna feeding near the surface. Outriggers (long poles to spread fishing lines far apart) stand tall on the port and starboard sides, and there are also many other smaller trolling stations in the stern to hold a battery of deep sea rods trolled at different depths. All rods are rigged and ready for action, and once it starts, there is a sturdy fish fighting chair bolted to the deck, complete with a harness to strap the fisherman in. *Sea Smoke* was well designed to handle tall waves and strong winds. But the captain, a native New Englander, wasn't familiar with southern waters. He cruised back and forth watching his sonar and scanned the surface ahead with his eyes in a futile search for a school of ballyhoo to net and fill his boat's empty bait well. Ballyhoo are small, beaked fish closely related to flying fish and are a favored food of big tuna, sailfish, and marlin. We couldn't catch the big fish without first catching the little ballyhoo for bait.

Our rods were light and rigged with small pieces of dead fish, which was all the bait the captain had on board and which dragged lifelessly in the boat's wake. Needless to say, we hadn't had a bite. It was me, my son-in-law Chuck—the embarrassed mate who had unwittingly signed on for a day with a clueless captain—and the captain, all watching the water for the sparkle and flash of ballyhoo.

In the sky, I spotted the dark distant shapes of frigate birds circling and diving. Frigate birds live most of their lives in the air over the ocean, landing on their small, rather weak feet only when coming to shore to rest. Their feathers, which are not waterproof, never touch the water.

At sea frigate birds flap, glide, soar, and hover, in a constant search for the same sparkle and flash that we were looking for. But when the birds spot ballyhoo swimming in the water below, they can't just dive down and get them. Their feathers would quickly become waterlogged, and their small feet could not propel them under water. They have to wait until some bigger fish show up and begin to feed, slashing through the schools, killing and maiming many fish before gobbling them down. The attacked fish that escape being eaten float helplessly to the surface. And it is these floating fish, some mortally wounded, some simply dazed, that the frigate birds feast on, scooping the casualties up off the waves with their long sharply hooked bills. Seeing a flock of frigate birds excitedly feeding on the surface always means big fish are feeding down below.

"Frigates!" I shouted, pointing to the birds in the distance.

"Change tackle!" the captain called to his mate. And in the next minutes the mood on board shifted from despair at not being able to catch even the smallest fish in the sea to excitement about the possibility of hooking into one of the biggest.

The mate hurried to replace the light flexible rods and light monofilament lines with a battery of stiff, big game rods. The big reels, spooled to capacity with heavy braided nylon lines, had wire tippets to absorb the shock of impact from a super-sized fish like a sailfish, wahoo, yellowfin, marlin, or humongous shark. The mate worked frantically to attach extra large hooks and dress them, carefully covering the hook points and barbs as well as he could with all the bait we had left. As the captain raced the boat full speed toward the frigates, Chuck and I held on to the rail, nervous but ready, like boxers in a ring, anticipating the fight of their lives.

The captain thought he saw the long bill and broad dorsal fin of a sailfish momentarily poke up out of a wave. We were all seeing things—sea turtles, dolphins, whole squadrons of flying fish. Our imaginations were running in high gear. But by the time we reached the hot spot, the frigate birds were gone. The feeding frenzy was over. However, overriding our disappointment at missing all the action was the sudden and awesome realization that we were in the presence of one of the world's great natural phenomena. The big black frigate birds had led us to the Gulf Stream!

The water there was blue-black, almost purple. And its powerful northerly flow was clearly evident. It looked like the river of all rivers. Its strong current ran up against the wave action coming from the shore, causing pieces of driftwood, matted seaweed, broken wooden planks, sheets of plywood, as well as Styrofoam cups and other floating trash that had drifted out from the land to bunch together in a long flotilla of junk stretching north and south as far as we could see. The endless line of debris bumped up to but did not break into the Stream's powerful flow.

Sea Smoke didn't break into the Stream either. The captain kept us cruising just outside within casting distance of any fish that might be lurking under the shelf of floating junk. By now our bait was stale and falling off the hooks. But I did manage to catch a large kingfish and Chuck caught a monster-sized barracuda with a head and tooth-filled jaws as long as those of an adult alligator.

When the captain found a break in the line of flotsam, he slipped the boat through into the dark water, throttling up to keep us going faster than the current so we wouldn't be carried off by it. The move made the hair on my neck bristle. We had left familiar water and crossed over into something else, where the biggest, most ferocious fish in the sea hunt, ever hungry, and we were on the menu! In the ocean you always know that there are dangerous fish in the water. But in the Gulf Stream, you become keenly aware of the fact that you too are a part of the ocean's food chain. All of a sudden *Sea Smoke* didn't seem so big and safe as it once did.

We fished in the strong northward current until our bait was gone. Then our captain pulled away from the Stream by slipping through another gap in the trash line and powering toward shore. *Sea Smoke* sliced through brilliant cobalt blue offshore waves, cruised in the clear water over the colorful coral reef, and glided back into the lime green water of the continental shelf. We hadn't found the super fish we sought, but we were in the right neighborhood—the great blue-black river in the sea, the Gulf Stream.

9.

"Old Blue Oars"

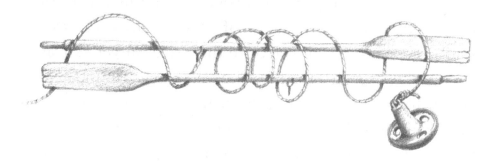

I have only been involved in one rescue at sea. It happened on Lake Champlain one cold and very blustery October day. The waves, whipped into whitecaps from the relentless push of a strong southerly wind, were dangerously high. *Old Blue Oars*, my beat-up, old, thirteen-foot aluminum rowboat with a four-horsepower outboard motor, was bobbing and rocking with the wind, tugging on its lines and banging its side repeatedly against our tiny dock. I had never seen the lake so dangerously wild. Looking through the binoculars, I scanned the water a few miles offshore, trying to estimate the height of the waves. Some looked to be six feet high.

When I first spotted the white sail of a boat heeling way over in those waves, I couldn't believe my eyes. "Who would be out in such weather?" I wondered. Focusing my binoculars on the vessel, I saw two either very brave or very foolish sailors on board. I kept the binoculars trained on their progress as their boat's bow rose high with the waves and slammed down in the troughs. The small wooden sloop's single mast carried a mainsail which was reefed down to a tiny triangle of cloth. Sailors reef their sails (fold them down to reduce their size) in very strong winds when a fully hoisted sail could catch too much air and be torn apart or worse, strain and break the mast. But even with its sail reefed to as small a triangle as possible, the wooden sloop was being blown way too far over onto its side. Water was flooding in over the rail, and it looked as though the boat might sink. Suddenly the wooden mast snapped and, after briefly foundering, the boat rolled completely over.

What was I to do? I could see the two sailors, neither man wearing a life jacket, in the water clinging to the capsized hull. They needed help right away. Left alone, they could float for miles in very cold water before reaching any shore. I scanned the waves hoping to see some other boat heading their way. But the sailors were alone out there and their capsized boat was now almost invisible amid the mounting waves. I had no radio to call the Coast Guard, and even if I did, by the time they made the thirty-mile trip up the lake from

Burlington, the men would have been in the cold water much too long. I explained to Deanna what was happening and then ran down to *Old Blue Oars* to start and warm up the engine.

There is a rule among boaters. If you see another boat in distress, you help if you can. Over the years, I've helped others afloat by throwing them a line and towing them in. But this was the first and so far only time I've ever attempted a bona fide rescue at sea. And what a sea it was! When Lake Champlain is calm it is as peaceful as a farm pond. When it is windy and rough, it can be as treacherous as a stormy ocean.

The outboard's tiny one-gallon gas tank was nearly full. I pulled on my life jacket and threw a couple in the boat for the two sailors. Then, filled with uncertainty and dread about the task before me, I untied the lines and pushed *Old Blue Oars* away from the dock. Turning slowly into the wind, I motored away from shore at full speed toward the capsized sailboat, now well over two miles away.

Two miles is a long distance on the water, especially when your boat's top speed is ten miles per hour, five in a strong headwind. All I could do to ease my fear was remind myself that because Deanna was watching from shore, unlike the stranded sailors out in the cold water, I knew someone was aware of my predicament.

Old Blue Oars' bow was lifted frighteningly high by each oncoming wave but the heavy gauge aluminum came down gently in the troughs. There was no hard pounding on the water. To make it ride even more smoothly and ensure that the boat wouldn't flip over, I sat forward on my seat to get my weight as near the center of the boat as I could, and still be able to reach the tiller. The engine ran steadily and its long shaft kept the prop down in the water pushing nicely. But I was only a quarter of a mile out.

At a half-mile out, everything changed. The waves increased from two to three feet, and the tiny engine just barely pushed the heavy boat over them. I really had to twist the throttle, revving the engine to maximum to make each wave, after which the bow pounded down so hard in the troughs that cold water splashed in. The water coming into the boat accumulated in a puddle that flowed aft when the hull rose, and forward when the hull came splashing back down. With each rise of the bow more water swirled and pooled around my feet.

A mile out, I thought I heard the tiny motor stalling out, but it was only the prop momentarily heaving up out of a high lifting wave causing the engine's water cooling intakes to suck air. The waves were now at least four feet high, and even the outboard's extra long shaft couldn't keep the propeller completely submerged 100 percent of the time. The water intakes momentarily sucking air made a coughing, sputtering sound similar to an engine running out of gas. Gas! I had forgotten about how much gas I was using. I quickly checked the little gas tank and found that, running at full throttle, the motor was using the gallon of gas up much faster than usual. If the engine ran out of fuel, there would be two boats dead in the water, at the mercy of the waves.

To save gas and still be able to make it over the on-coming waves, I tried surfing the boat in the troughs. After climbing over a wave, I turned to the right and skidded or surfed inside the trough to gather momentum before turning into the next wave, to get up and over and back on course. At one point, as *Old Blue Oars* slid high over a wave, I caught sight of the men still clinging to their up-turned boat. They must have seen me coming because one of them began waving wildly.

My plan was to get close enough to the capsized boat to be able to throw the sailors the life jackets. Then I'd pick them up one at a time. But to my horror, when I was still over a hundred yards away, they left their vessel and began swimming toward me! I shuddered to think that my attempt to rescue them could end in tragedy. They had already been in the cold water enough time for them to be experiencing hypothermia. Now, encouraged by the sight of rescue, they were attempting an Olympic-distance swim that could deplete whatever body heat they had left!

I raced *Old Blue Oars* toward the men to make the distance they would have to swim as short as possible. When we were within shouting range, I told them I was going to cruise close enough for each, one at a time, to climb aboard. The first sailor I came to had enough strength to pull himself over the gunwale of my boat. The second was sinking when we reached him and it took a great effort for two of us to pull him, completely exhausted, up and in.

Their boat was a wreck. The broken mast floated, still attached to the mainstays which were loosely rapping against the hull in rhythm to the pounding waves. The capsized hull shone like the shell of a great turtle surfacing in a storm. The sail, its reefing all unfurled, was shredded and waving, ghost-like in the water. I felt awful for the boat and for the two men. But they had survived.

The man who had to be pulled out of the water sat shivering with his head hanging down, and his hands folded on his lap. His companion stared silently back at the floating wreckage. He too was shaking and shivering. Neither man had much energy to speak, so I didn't ask questions and left them to their thoughts.

Old Blue Oars cradled us all comfortably and the added ballast of two passengers made the boat ride more smoothly over the waves. Running homeward with the wind at our stern used much less gas than the trip out, and *Old Blue Oars* kept going all the way back to shore, like a reliable and trustworthy horse after a strenuous ride, heading straight for the stable.

After many years of hard use *Old Blue Oars*' transom began to leak beyond repair. These days the old boat rests on the shore of the lake where I often sit on its upturned hull to rig my rods, sketch the shoreline, or play my guitar near the water. Sometimes I just sit and recall the times the old boat and I spent on the water together, and I remember the two sailors who survived their capsizing in frigid water because *Old Blue Oars* was seaworthy enough to get to them and carry us all back safely to shore.

Epilogue

In old boats and new, in chartered vessels with captain and crew, or in our own beloved boats, Deanna and I have sailed, motored, paddled, and rowed over ten thousand miles to get to where we wanted to be on the water. For us, thousands of miles comprised of one-, two-, ten-, twenty-, and fifty-mile trips have added up to a lifelong adventure filled with discovery, exploration, understanding, and appreciation of our watery world. All of this lies in the open water, just waiting for you to sail through.

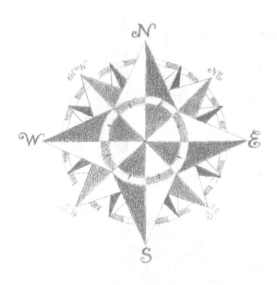

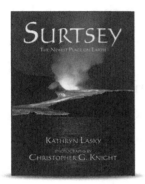 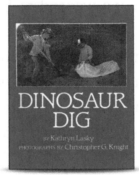 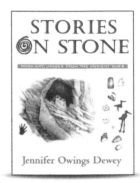

CPSIA information can be obtained at www.ICGtesting.com
Printed in the USA
BVOW10s1840090514

353054BV00009B/27/P